espresso
education

Phonics

The Run-Away Game

Gill Budgell

W
FRANKLIN WATTS
LONDON•SYDNEY

First published in 2012 by
Franklin Watts
338 Euston Road
London NW1 3BH

Franklin Watts Australia
Level 17/207 Kent Street
Sydney NSW 2000

The Espresso characters are originated and designed by Claire Underwood and Pesky Ltd.

The Espresso characters are the property of Espresso Education Ltd.

A CIP catalogue record for this book is available from the British Library.

ISBN: 978 1 4451 0749 3 (hbk)
ISBN: 978 1 4451 0752 3 (pbk)

Illustrations by Artful Doodlers Ltd.
Art Director: Jonathan Hair
Series Editor: Jackie Hamley
Project Manager: Gill Budgell
Series Designer: Matthew Lilly

Printed in China

Franklin Watts is a division of
Hachette Children's Books,
an Hachette UK company.

www.hachette.co.uk

Level 1 50 words
Concentrating on CVC words plus and, the, to

Level 2 70 words
Concentrating on double letter sounds and new letter sounds (ck, ff, ll, ss, j, v, w, x, y, z, zz) plus no, go, I

Level 3 100 words
Concentrating on new graphemes (qu, ch, sh, th, ng, ai, ee, igh, oa, oo, ar, or, ur, ow, oi, ear, air, ure, er) plus he, she, we, me, be, was, my, you, they, her, all

Level 4 150 words
Concentrating on adjacent consonants (CVCC/CCVC words) plus said, so, have, like, some, come, were, there, little, one, do, when, out, what

Level 5 180 words
Concentrating on new graphemes (ay, wh, ue, ir, ou, aw, ph, ew, ea, a-e, e-e, i-e, o-e, u-e) plus day, very, put, time, about, saw, here, came, made, don't, asked, looked, called, Mrs

Level 6 200 words
Concentrating on alternative pronunciations (c, ow, o, g, y) and spellings (ee, ur, ay, or, m, n, air, l, r) plus your, don't time, saw, here, very, make, their, called, asked, looked

Ash and Eddy took Scrap
and Scully out for a run.

"Take them off the lead,"
said Ash.

He threw a
stick for them.
It was a good
game.

"Here Scully!" shouted Ash.
"Leave it now, Scrap!"
called Eddy.

But the dogs did not
even look back.

Scully ran on.

Scrap saw a duck.
"Don't chase the duck!"
called Eddy.

Oh dear!

The duck flew away
but Scrap ran on.

The dogs saw some thick
sticky mud.
"Please stay out of the mud.
Keep clean!" shouted Ash.

Scrap and Scully ran on.
They went over a gate

and came to a stream.

15

Scrap went splash!

Scully went splash!

The boys got to the stream.
"I can leap over it!" said Ash.

Ash flew along but…

Splash!

Scrap and Scully came back.
Eddy got them on the lead.
"No more 'run-away game'
for you!" he said.

Oh dear!

Puzzle Time

Find the six sound pairs!
One has been done for you.

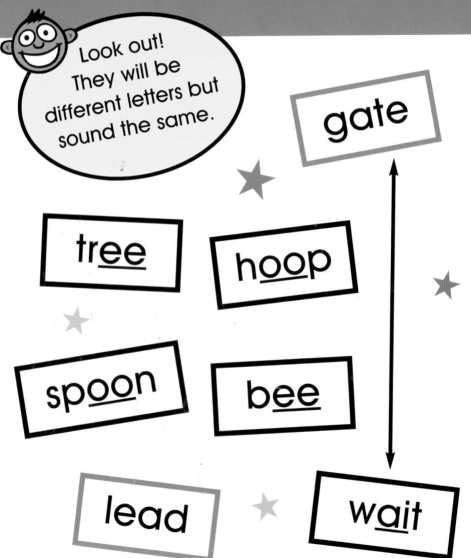

Look out! They will be different letters but sound the same.

gate

tree

hoop

spoon

bee

lead

wait

screw

even

m<u>ai</u>l

flew

chase

Answers

wait – gate is already completed to show the first pair.

chase and **mail** are also both **/ai/**
bee, tree, even, lead are all **/ee/**
hoop, flew, screw, spoon are all long **/oo/**

A note about the phonics in this book

Concentrating on new phonemes

In this book children practise reading new graphemes (letters) for some phonemes (sounds) that they already know. For example, they already know that the letters ee make the /ee/ sound but now they are practising that ea and e-e can also make the /ee/ sound.

Known phoneme	New graphemes	Words in the story
/ai/	a-e	came, chase, late, gate, take
/ee/	ea	stream, please, lead, leave, leap, clean
/ee/	e-e	these, even
/oo/ .	ew	threw, chew, flew
common words	here, came, don't	
tricky common words	called	

Remind children about the letters they already know for these phonemes.

In the puzzle they are challenged to match the words that have the same sound in them; the same sound but different letters.

Top tip: if a child gets stuck on a word then ask them to try and sound it out and then blend it together again or show them how to do this. For example, stream, s-t-r-ea-m, stream.

24

th